Praise for Elin Hilderbrand's

The Rumor

"Hilderbrand is the queen of the summer beach read."
—Thomas Farragher, *Boston Globe*

"It wouldn't be summer without a breezy, sensual Nantucket tale from Hilderbrand, and her latest—about two families and some damaging gossip—doesn't disappoint. Intricately plotted and filled with fast-paced dialogue, it's as sweetly satisfying as a glass of Sancerre."
—Kim Hubbard, *People*

"The detail is authentic....Expect to find *The Rumor* filled with all the ingredients of a great chick-lit read: many characters with intertwined lives, a handsome guy (in this case, a landscape architect), complicated romance, and lots of wine."
—Georgea Kovanis, *Detroit Free Press*

"Hilderbrand has become synonymous with the perfect summer beach read, and *The Rumor* should find its way into many beach bags. Readers will be hooked as they get a glimpse into the messy lives of the beautiful people who only seem to have it all on this island."
—*Library Journal*

"Explores human nature and the truth behind the gossip that people love to be the first to share."
—Laurie Higgins, *The Cape Codder*

"Elin Hilderbrand, queen of the romance novel, never disappoints her readers—and here she is at the top of her game once again. She details every character superbly, her themes and plotlines are well thought out, and you can picture every scene in your mind so vividly. I read *The Rumor* quickly because I needed to know what ultimately happens and had no idea how it was going to end.... Rumor has it that you will enjoy this book as much as I did."

—Vivian Payton, BookReporter.com

ALSO BY ELIN HILDERBRAND

The Rumor

A Novel

Elin Hilderbrand

Little, Brown and Company

New York • Boston • London

Little, Brown and Company
Hachette Book Group
1290 Avenue of the Americas
New York, NY 10104
littlebrown.com

Little, Brown and Company is a division of Hachette Book Group, Inc. The Little, Brown and Company name and logo is a trademark of Hachette Book Group, Inc.

Printed in the United States of America

Originally published in hardcover by Little, Brown and Company, June 2015
First Little, Brown and Company mass market edition, July 2016

10 9 8 7 6 5 4 3 2 1

It is with the humblest gratitude that I dedicate this book to
Dr. Michelle Specht, for saving my life,
and to
Dr. Amy Colwell, for saving my body.
#mamastrong